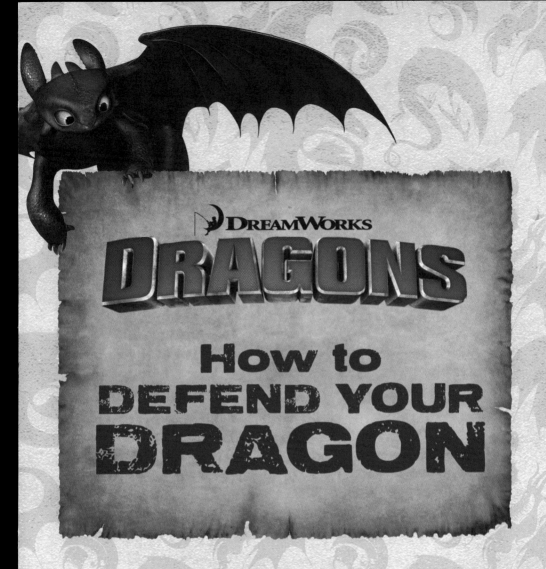

DreamWorks
DRAGONS

How to
DEFEND YOUR
DRAGON

adapted by Ellie O'Ryan

Ready-to-Read

Simon Spotlight

New York   London   Toronto   Sydney   New Delhi

In this story, while Hiccup is trying to help Toothless, he stays outside during a lightning storm. This is very dangerous, and in real life you should never be outside when you see lightning, even if it seems far away. If you see lightning when you are outside, you should find shelter immediately. Remember, you don't have a dragon to protect you—stay safe!

SIMON SPOTLIGHT
An imprint of Simon & Schuster Children's Publishing Division
1230 Avenue of the Americas, New York, New York 10020
First Simon Spotlight edition May 2015
DreamWorks Dragons © 2015 DreamWorks Animation LLC.
For information about special discounts for bulk purchases, please contact Simon & Schuster Special Sales at
1-866-506-1949 or business@simonandschuster.com.
Manufactured in the United States of America 0415 LAK
2 4 6 8 10 9 7 5 3 1
ISBN 978-1-4814-3710-3 (pbk)
ISBN 978-1-4814-3711-0 (hc)
ISBN 978-1-4814-3713-4 (eBook)

Living with dragons can be great—
but it is not always easy.
Some are so big that when they land
on the roof, the house falls down!

Hiccup knows what to do.
First he draws some plans.
Then the Vikings build metal perches
for the dragons.

Will Hiccup's idea work?
Stormfly soars toward the perch.
Then she lands on it!
"Yes!" cheers Hiccup.

Dark clouds race across the sky.
A storm is brewing—a big storm.
Thunder booms. Lightning strikes.
"Whoa," Hiccup says. "The lightning
is hitting everywhere!"
The Vikings are worried.
They think when lightning strikes
that the god Thor is angry.

Stoick and Gobber remember the
last time lightning hit the village.
They thought Thor was punishing
a thief. When the Vikings sent the
thief away, the lightning stopped.

But why is Thor mad now?
Maybe if the Vikings can learn
the answer, they can keep the
village safe.

Crack! Boom!
More lightning strikes.
One bolt almost hits Toothless!

Many houses are burning.
The Vikings and the dragons work
together to put out the fires.
At last the storm ends.
But fixing the damage has just
begun.

Mildew points at Toothless.
"Thor is angry with us because of the Night Fury," he shouts.
Mildew tells everyone that they must send Toothless away.
He says that is the only way to keep the village safe.

Hiccup knows that Mildew is wrong.
He has got to come up with another
plan. But what?

"If I were Thor, I would want
a giant statue," Snotlout says.
Hiccup thinks that is a great idea!
Everyone works hard to build
a huge statue of Thor.
The metal statue shines in the sun.
"I really think Thor is going to like
this!" says Hiccup.

Everyone is impressed—except
Mildew. He still wants to send
Toothless away.
"You are fools, all of you!"
Mildew yells.

Suddenly, the sky grows dark.
A new storm is coming.
It is even bigger than the last one!
More lightning strikes the houses
and the perches. Some bolts even hit
the new statue of Thor.

Tuffnut and Ruffnut love
watching the storm wreck things.
"Nobody blows stuff up like Thor!"
Tuffnut says.

Everyone can see that the statue
did not work.
Mildew convinces the others
to get rid of Toothless.
They march to Hiccup's house.

"Get Toothless to a safe place,"
Stoick tells Hiccup.
Hiccup does not want Toothless
to go away.
But he is determined to protect
his friend.

When Stoick opens the door,
Mildew says, "Give up the dragon!"
"You are too late," says Stoick.
"He is gone."

Mildew refuses to give up.
"Find the Night Fury!" he orders.

Meanwhile, Hiccup and Toothless
fly into the clouds.
A new storm is brewing—
and it's a big one.

Toothless tries to dodge the
lightning, but one bolt strikes his
metal tail fin.
The dragon spins out of control!

Hiccup and Toothless crash
in the forest.
"You okay, bud?" Hiccup asks.
Toothless will be fine, but the metal
on his tail fin is still glowing.

"That is where the lightning hit," Hiccup realizes. He remembers how lightning struck the metal statue and the metal perches, too.

Just then Mildew and the villagers find them. They capture Toothless and take him to the dock.

They want to send Toothless away
forever!
This is Hiccup's last chance
to save his friend.

Hiccup points up at the sky. "The lightning is hitting the metal," Hiccup explains.

Then the lightning hits more metal,
and Hiccup is knocked down
by the force of the lightning strike.
He falls in the water!

Toothless breaks free and dives
into the ocean. He grabs Hiccup
and swims for the surface as fast
as he can.

When Hiccup finally wakes up,
he does not remember anything.

Stoick explains how Hiccup proved that the lightning was only hitting metal objects.
Thor was not angry at Toothless.
Now Toothless does not have to leave!

Now everyone in Berk
knows what Hiccup has known
all along.
There is no better friend
in the world than Toothless!